SESAME STREET

FRIENDLY, FROSTY MONSTERS

S0-AII-802

By P.J. Shaw
Sketches by Tom Brannon
Colorization by Joel Schick

Dalmatian KIDS

Published by Dalmatian Kids, an imprint of Dalmatian Publishing Group, LLC. The DALMATIAN KIDS name and logo are trademarks of Dalmatian Publishing Group, LLC, Franklin, Tennessee 37067. No part of this book may be reproduced or copied in any form without written permission from the copyright owner.

Printed in the U.S.A.
ISBN: 1-40373-709-6 (M) 1-40373-612-X (X)

07 08 09 10 NGS 10 9 8 7 6 5 4 3 2
16274 Sesame Street 8x8 Storybook: Friendly, Frosty Monsters

"Yay! Yippee! It's a monstrously snowy day on Sesame Street!"

On with snowsuits and rubber boots. Sometimes you need a big brother—or Big Bird—to help.

Zip and clip!

Clasp and snap!

Wiggle, waggle, tussle, tug!

Slippery-slide on skiddy skates.
Watch out or you'll wobble!

"Oh, dear! Oh, no!" weeps Little Bo-Peep.
"My wooly white sheep ran away in the snow!
Where did they go?"

Run and romp!

Baaaa

Slide
and
stomp!

Can you help find all ten?
Plus one shivery black sheep!

Baby Bear slides happily down the hill!
Jack and Jill come tumbling after.

Whish, swish, vroom!

Flitter

Flutter

Float

Softly f - a - l - l

In a wintry wood, Red Riding Hood
enjoys a walk with Bert.
(But beware of that watchful wolf!)

Making friendly, frosty monsters is easy if you try. Big button eyes—with a snazzy schnoz or a frosty frown.

Pat! Pack!

Roll it 'round!

Off with boots, hats, and monster mittens. Inside for songs— and milk for the three little kittens.